I'd Rather Be a FOOTBALLER

The very best of Paul Cookson

When Paul was at school, he would have rather been a footballer than anything else – especially if it meant playing for Everton! A second choice would have been to play rock-and-roll guitar for a band like Slade. Instead, he wrote poems and became a poet.

Since 1989 he has worked as a poet, performing thousands of shows at thousands of schools and publishing over forty collections of children's poetry, including *The Works*, *Pants on Fire* and *Give Us a Goal*.

He is now the Poet-in-Residence at the National Football Museum and Poet Laureate for Slade, and his work has appeared regularly on national radio and television. Paul lives in Retford with Sally, Sam and Daisy – and Max the dog.

If he has any spare time he likes to play five-a-side football, read too many books, buy too many CDs, watch Everton play and practise his ukulele (but not all at the same time!).

David Parkins has illustrated numerous books, ranging from maths textbooks to the *Beano*. His picture books have been shortlisted for the Smarties Book Prize and the Kurt Maschler Award. He lives in Lincoln with his wife, three children and six cats.

I'd Rather Be a FOOTBALLER

The very best of Paul Cookson

Illustrated by David Parkins

MACMILLAN CHILDREN'S BOOKS

Dedicated to Richard, Xanthe, Gabriel and Isaac
And the Potato 5 extended family.
So much to remember

First published 2008 by Macmillan Children's Books
a division of Macmillan Publishers Limited
20 New Wharf Road, London N1 9RR
Basingstoke and Oxford
Associated companies throughout the world
www.panmacmillan.com

ISBN 978-0-330-45713-2

1 3 5 7 9 8 6 4 2

A CIP catalogue record for this book is available from
the British Library.

Typeset by Nigel Hazle
Printed and bound in China

Contents

I'd Rather Be a Footballer

Stuck in class doing maths
Staring at the wall
I'd rather be a footballer
Kicking my football

I'll blast it and I'll pass it
Leave them feeling small
I'd rather be a footballer
Kicking my football

I'll flick it up and kick it up
Beating one and all
I'd rather be a footballer
Kicking my football

I'll dribble it then middle it
Score the goals to take us up
I wannabe in Wembley
Score and win the FA Cup

I can't ignore the call
I'm setting out my stall
I'd rather be a footballer
A legendary footballer
Kicking my football

1

Coolscorin' Matchwinnin' Celebratin' Striker!

I'm a shirt removin' crowd salutin'
handstandin' happy landin'
rockin' rollin' divin' slidin'
posin' poutin' loud shoutin'
pistol packin' smoke blowin'
flag wavin' kiss throwin'
hipswingin' armwavin'
breakdancin' cool ravin'
shoulder shruggin' team huggin'
hot shootin' rootin' tootin'
somersaultin' fence vaultin'
last-minute goal grinnin'
shimmy shootin' shin spinnin'
celebratin' cup   winnin' STRIKER!

The Footballer's Prayer

Let us play . . .

Our team
Which art eleven
Hallowed be thy game
Our match be won
Their score be none
On turf – as we score at least seven
Give us today
No daily red card
And forgive us our lost passes
As we forgive those
Who lose passes against us
Lead us not into retaliation
And deliver us from penalties
For three is the kick off
The power and the scorer
For ever and ever
Full time

He Just Can't Kick It with His Foot

John Luke from our team
Is a goal-scoring machine
Phenomenally mesmerizing but . . .
The sport is called football
But his boots don't play at all
Cos he just can't kick it with his foot

He can skim it from his shin
He can spin it on his chin
He can nod it in the net with his nut
He can blow it with his lips
Or skip it off his hips
But he just can't kick it with his foot

With simplicity and ease
He can use his knobbly knees
To blast it past the keeper, both eyes shut
He can whip it up and flick it
With his tongue and lick it
But he still can't kick it with his foot

Overshadowing the best
With the power from his chest
Like a rocket from a socket he can put
The ball into the sack
With a scorcher from his back
But he just can't kick it with his foot

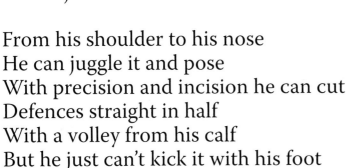

Baffling belief
With the ball between his teeth
He can dribble his way out of any rut
Hypnotize it with his eyes
Keep it up on both his thighs
But he just can't kick it with his foot

From his shoulder to his nose
He can juggle it and pose
With precision and incision he can cut
Defences straight in half
With a volley from his calf
But he just can't kick it with his foot

He can keep it off the deck
Bounce the ball upon his neck
With his ball control you should see him strut
He can flap it with both ears
To loud applause and cheers
But he just can't kick it with his foot

He can trap it with his tum
Direct it with his bum
Deflect it just by wobbling his gut
When he's feeling silly
He can even use his . . . ankle!
But he just can't kick it with his foot

The Goalie with Expanding Hands

Any crosses, any shots
I will simply stop the lot
I am always in demand
The goalie with expanding hands

Volleys, blasters, scissor kicks
I am safe between the sticks
All attacks I will withstand
The goalie with expanding hands

Free kicks or a penalty
No one ever scores past me
Strong and bold and safe I'll stand
The goalie with expanding hands

Let their strikers be immense
I'm the last line of defence
Alert, on duty, all posts manned
The goalie with expanding hands

Palms as long as arms expand
Thumbs and fingers ready fanned
You may as well shoot in the stand
Not a chance! Understand?
Number one in all the land
Superhuman, super-spanned
In control and in command
I'm the man, I'm the man
The one and only goalie . . . with my expanding hands

Lest We Forget

Remember not the tragedy, the shadows of the memory,
The sadness and the sense of waste but the one you used to be

The majesty and trickery, the entertaining joy,
The impish smile and twinkling eyes of Belfast's golden boy

The stardom and the skill, the quick and dancing feet,
Audacious with both left and right, inventive and complete

You touched our lives with magic and gave us all a dream,
You, the one we tried to be when playing for our team

A genius on the pitch, you stood above the rest,
Poetry in motion, George – you were the Best.

Losing at Home

I never really cried when my grandma died.
You see, I was away from home at the time.
The first time I saw my grandfather afterwards
he was watching World Cup football on the telly.
He told me that it was a good match and that
the goalkeeper had made some fantastic saves
although we were still one nil down.
But somewhere behind his eyes
a light had dimmed
and on the other side of his glasses
I could see teardrops forming
and as they fell down his face
they weren't because his team had lost
but because he had lost
his team.

You see, to my grandfather
my grandmother was his best team
in the world.
Ever.

Professor McBoffin's Amazing Creations

Self-cleaning socks for long-distance runners
Self-cooling sandals for steaming-hot summers
Bedsocks for dogs, fatter pillows for cats
Spring-loaded exocet-strength cricket bats
Self-inflating lifesaving knickers
Pulpits with engines for overworked vicars
All these and more – the newest sensations
Professor McBoffin's amazing creations!

Bananas and oranges fitted with zips
Healthy calorie-free fish and chips
Centrally heated warm toilet seats
Non-flavour-fading non-shrinking sweet sweets
A homework computer that fits in the pocket
Football boots with the power of a rocket
All these and more – the newest sensations
Professor McBoffin's amazing creations!

With sprockets and sockets and test tubes that boil
Wires and fires, foil and oil
Springs that go zing and things that uncoil
Professor McBoffin's all trial and toil

Jottings and workings and odd calculations
Diagrams labelled with weird notations
Models that move with the strangest rotations
Professor McBoffin knows no limitations

A brain and a mind beyond contemplation
Professor McBoffin's amazing creations!

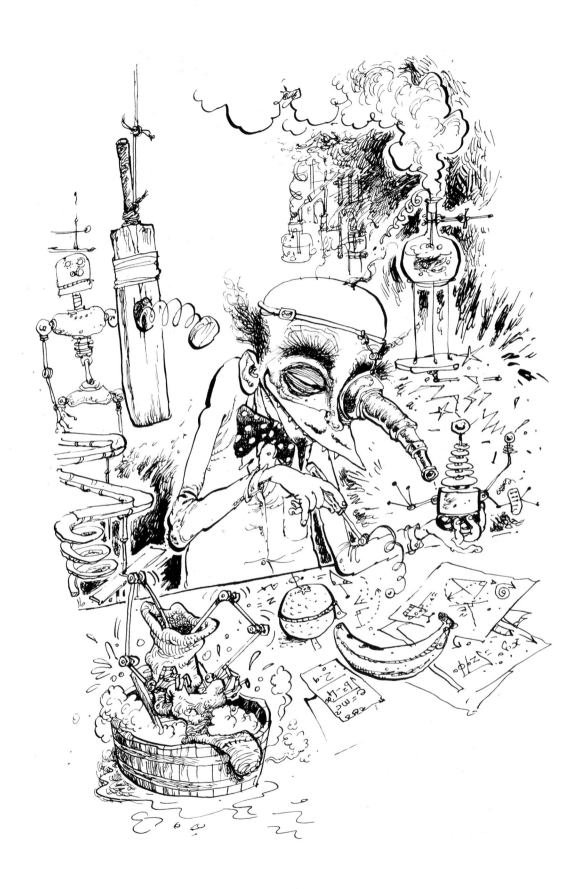

Barry and Beryl
the Bubblegum Blowers

Barry and Beryl the bubblegum blowers
blew bubblegum bubbles as big as balloons.
All shapes and sizes, zebras and zeppelins,
swordfish and sea lions, sharks and baboons,
babies and buckets, bottles and biplanes,
buffaloes, bees, trombones and bassoons.
Barry and Beryl the bubblegum blowers
blew bubblegum bubbles as big as balloons.

Barry and Beryl the bubblegum blowers
blew bubblegum bubbles all over the place.
Big ones in bed, on back seats of buses,
blowing their bubbles in baths with bad taste,
they blew and they bubbled from breakfast till bedtime
the biggest gum bubble that history traced.
One last big breath . . . and the bubble exploded,
bursting and blasting their heads into space.
Yes, Barry and Beryl the bubblegum blowers
blew bubbles that blasted their heads into space.

Superman's Dog

Superman's dog – he's the best
Helping pets in distress
Red-and-gold pants and vest
'SD' on his chest

Superman's dog – X-ray sight
Green bones filled with Kryptonite
Bright blue Lycra tights in flight
Faster than a meteorite

Better than Batman's robin
Rougher than Robin's bat
Faster than Spiderman's spider
Cooler than Catwoman's cat

Superman's dog – bionic scent
Crime prevention – his intent
Woof and tough – cement he'll dent
What's his name – Bark Kent!

The Evil Doctor Mucus Spleen

Who schemes an evil scheming scheme?
Who dreams an evil dreaming dream?
Who wants to rule the world supreme?
Who has the evillest inventions?
Who has the evillest intentions?
Thoughts and plans too dark to mention . . .
The Evil Evil Evil . . . Dr Mucus Spleen!

Who's the crime at every scene?
Who wants to turn the whole world green?
Who's not ozone-friendly clean?
His phaser laser quasar blaster
Blasts his poison ever faster
Emerald phlegm in quick-dry plaster
The Evil Evil Evil . . . Dr Mucus Spleen!

Whose operations and routines
Take science to the dark extremes?
Who's part alien, part machine?
His cauldrons bubble, test tubes fizz
Sockets hum and wires whizz
I bet you know just who it is . . .
The Evil Evil Evil . . . Dr Mucus Spleen!

Whose habits are the most obscene?
Whose toes are full of jam between?
Whose armpits boil and trousers steam?
Who drips slime and goo and ooze?
Who smells of ancient sweat-stained shoes?
Who's the baddest of bad news?
The Evil Evil Evil . . . Dr Mucus Spleen!

He's mean! He's green! He'll make you scream!
The baddest villain ever seen!
Watch out for his laser beam!
The Evil Evil Evil . . . Dr Mucus Spleen!

The Amazing Captain Concorde

5 4 3 2 1 . . . BLAST OFF!

Is it a bird? Is it a plane?
Look at the size of the nose on his face!
Is it a bird? Is it a plane?
Captain Concorde is his name!
Captain Concorde NEEOWN!
What a big nose NEEOWN!

He's a man with a mission
Radar vision
A nose that's supersonic
Faster than the speed of sound
His Y-fronts are bionic

Is it a bird? Is it a plane?
Look at the size of the nose on his face!
Is it a bird? Is it a plane?
Captain Concorde is his name!
Captain Concorde NEEOWN!
What a big nose NEEOWN!

Anytime anyplace anywhere
But never ever Mondays
Cos that's the day the Captain's mum
Washes his red undies.
Anytime anyplace anywhere
His power is fantastic
Everything's under control
With super-strength elastic!
Anytime anyplace anywhere
But bathrooms are a no-no
Cos the toilet seat has teeth! OW!
And then it's time to go so . . .

Is it a bird? Is it a plane?
Look at the size of the nose on his face!
Is it a bird? Is it a plane?
Captain Concorde is his name!
Captain Concorde NEEOWN!
What a big nose NEEOWN!

The Amazing Captain Concorde . . . he's a superman.
The Amazing Captain Concorde . . . super underpants.

Who's the man with the supersonic nose? . . . Captain Concorde!
Who's the man with the terrible taste in clothes? . . . Captain Concorde!
Who's the man who always helps his mum? . . . Captain Concorde!
Who's the man you'd like to become? . . . Captain Concorde!

Is it a bird? Is it a plane?
Look at the size of the nose on his face!
Is it a bird? Is it a plane?
Captain Concorde is his name!
Captain Concorde NEEOWN!
What a big nose NEEOWN!

Miss Smith's Mythical Bag

The curse of every class she'll see
No one knows its history
Its origin's a mystery
 . . . Miss Smith's Mythical Bag

Beyond our understanding
You dare not put your hand in
The bag that keeps expanding
. . . Miss Smith's Mythical Bag

Broken chalk, a thousand pens with red ink that's congealed,
Forgotten fungus-covered bread and mouldy orange peel,
Lost car keys and headache pills, a Roman spear and shield,
Football cards and marbles, the goalposts from the field.

Where she goes it follows
All rippling lumps and hollows
The strangest things it swallows
. . . Miss Smith's Mythical Bag

With a menacing unzipped grin it's
From the Outer Limits
There are black holes deep within it
. . . Miss Smith's Mythical Bag

Crinkled tissues, Blu-Tack balls, disfigured paper clips,
Sweets all covered up with fluff, dried up fibre tips,
Lumps of powdered milk and coffee, last year's fish and chips,
From the Triangle in Bermuda – several missing ships.

Sometimes you hear it groan
Beyond the Twilight Zone
Make sure you're not alone
. . . Miss Smith's Mythical Bag

Shape-shifting, changing sizes,
The bag she never tidies,
it metamorphosizes
. . . Miss Smith's Mythical Bag

More mysterious than Loch Ness, it's from the Fifth Dimension,
Stranger than an alien race beyond our comprehension,
Brooding with a strange intent that no one wants to mention,
You'd better pay attention or you'll be in detention

With Miss Smith's mythical, metaphysical,
astronomical, gastronomical, anatomical,
clinical, cynical bag!

The Toilet Seat Has Teeth

The bathroom has gone crazy
far beyond belief.
The sink is full of spiders
and the toilet seat has teeth!

The plughole in the bath
has a whirlpool underneath
that pulls you down feet first
and the toilet seat has teeth!

The toothpaste tube is purple
and makes your teeth fall out.
The toilet roll is nettles
and makes you scream and shout!

The towels have got bristles,
the bubble bath is glue,
the soap has turned to jelly
and it makes your skin bright blue.

The mirror's pulling faces
at everyone it can.
The shower's dripping marmalade
and blackcurrant jam.

The rubber ducks are breeding
and building their own nest
with shaving foam and tissues
in Grandad's stringy vest.

Shampoo is liquid dynamite,
there's petrol in the hairspray,
both will cure dandruff
when they blow your head away!

The bathroom has gone crazy
far beyond belief.
The sink is full of spiders
and the toilet seat has teeth!

The plughole in the bath
has a whirlpool underneath
that pulls you down feet first
and the toilet seat has teeth!

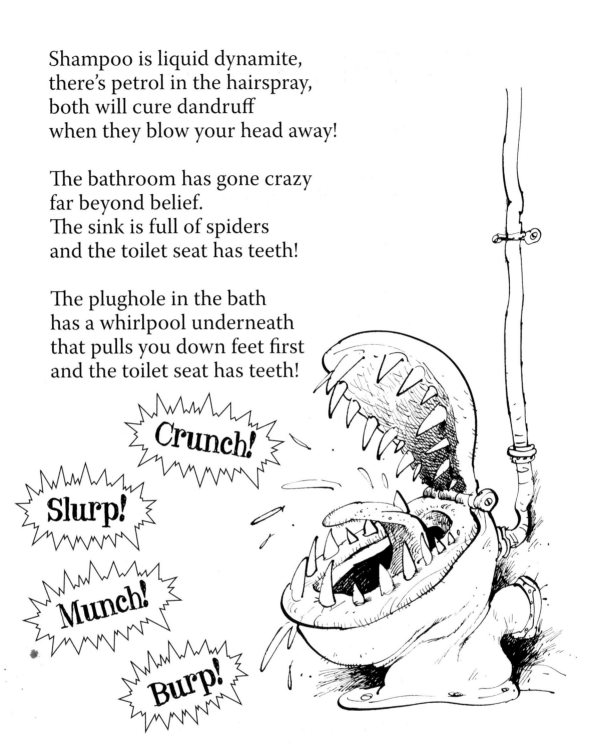

Crunch!

Slurp!

Munch!

Burp!

The toilet seat has teeth! Ow!
Don't – sit – on – it!
The toilet seat has . . . Owwwww!

We Are the Chompions!

We are the champs, we are the top
Of Premier Division One.
Nobody scores against us when
Our goalie is 'Big Bron'.

We're solid in defence
And cutting in attack,
Trexi's up the front
And Stego's at the back.

Terry D is on the wing
Unchallenged in the air,
The midfield wins with the twins
Vel and Ossie Rapto there.

We play with incision,
We always leave our mark,
We're Dinosaurs United
And our ground's Jurassic Park.

The King of All the Dinosaurs

With taloned feet and razor claws,
Leathery scales, monstrous jaws . . .
The king of all the dinosaurs
Tyrannosaurus rex.

With sabre teeth no one ignores,
It rants and raves and royally roars . . .
The king of all the dinosaurs
Tyrannosaurus rex.

The largest of all carnivores,
It stomps and chomps on forest floors . . .
The king of all the dinosaurs
Tyrannosaurus rex.

Charges forwards waging wars,
Gouges, gorges, gashes, gores . . .
The king of all the dinosaurs
Tyrannosaurus rex.

With taloned feet and razor claws,
Leathery scales, monstrous jaws,
Sabre teeth no one ignores,
It rants and raves and royally roars . . .
The king of all the dinosaurs
Tyrannosaurus rex.

Sea Shoals See Shows on the Sea Bed

The salmon with a hat on was conducting with a baton
And it tried to tune a tuna fish by playing on its scales
The scales had all been flattened when the tuna fish was sat on
On purpose by a porpoise and a school of killer whales.
So the salmon with a hat on fiddled with his baton
While the angelfish got ready to play the tambourine
Things began to happen when the salmon with a baton
Was tapping out a pattern for the band of the marines

There was a minnow on piano, a prawn with a horn,
An otter on guitar looking all forlorn,
A whale-voice choir and a carp with a harp,
A belly-dancing jellyfish jiving with a shark

The octaves on the octopus played the middle eight
But they couldn't keep in tune with the skiffle-playing skate
The plaice on the bass began to rock and roll
With the bloater on a boater and a Dover sole

A clam on castanets, an eel on glockenspiel,
An oyster in a cloister singing with a seal
The haddock had a headache from the deafening din
And the sword-dancing swordfish sliced off a fin

A limpet on a trumpet, flatfish on a flute
The kipper fell asleep with King Canute
Barracuda on a tuba sat upon a rock
The electric eel gave everyone a shock

The shrimp and the sturgeon, the stingray and the squid
Sang a four-part harmony on the sea bed
The crab and the lobster gave their claws a flick
Kept everyone in time with a click click click . . .
Kept everyone in time with a click click click . . .
Kept everyone in time with a click click click . . .

Yes, the salmon with a hat on was tapping out a pattern
And things began to happen for the band of the marines
It was an ocean of commotion of Atlantic proportion
The greatest show by schools of shoals that had ever been seen

The Model We're Making in Class with Miss

Scissors, glue, yogurt pots,
Sellotape, a cornflake box,
egg cartons, bottle tops,
rubber gloves, Dad's old socks

Cardboard, hardboard
and my brother's dartboard,
polythene, plasticine
and my mother's magazine

Walking sticks, building bricks,
lipsticks, Pritt Sticks,
silly string, safety pins,
lots and lots of other things

Plastic, elastic,
we're enthusiastic
mould it and fold it
then we'll plaster-cast it
mould it and fold it
it'll be fantastic

Add a bit of that, then a bit of this
for the model we're making in class with Miss
stick it on that, stick it on this
for the model we're making, the model we're making
the model we're making in class with Miss
the model we're making, the model we're making
the model we're making in class with . . . Miss.

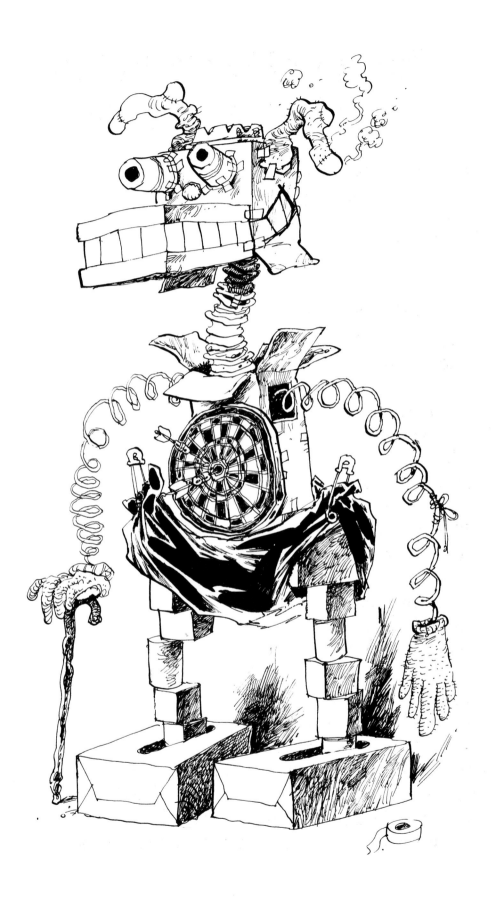

Bouncy Mr Springer

BOING! BOING! BA- DOING BOING BOING!

He bounces when he walks
And he bounces when he talks
He bounces down the corridor
Up and down on the school hall floor
Up and down on the school hall floor

BOING! BOING! BA- DOING BOING BOING!

Up and down he bounces round
And points his bouncy finger
Best watch out when he's about
It's bouncy Mr Springer

BOING! BOING! BA- DOING BOING BOING!

He bounces in assembly
His rubber knees are trembly
You can tell where he has been
He's a human trampoline
A jumping bean on a trampoline

BOING! BOING! BA- DOING BOING BOING!

A never-ending pogo stick
He's like a punk-rock singer
Best watch out when he's about
Bouncy Mr Springer

BOING! BOING! BA- DOING BOING BOING!

He bounces here, bounces there
And he bounces everywhere
Bounces on tables, bounces on chairs
Bounces on the playground and bounces down the stairs

BOING! BOING! BA- DOING BOING BOING!

He twitches like a wasp
That's got an awkward stinger
Best watch out when he's about
Bouncy Mr Springer

BOING! BOING! BA- DOING BOING BOING!

Billy Doesn't Like School Really

Billy doesn't like school really.
It's not because he can't do the work
but because some of the other kids
don't seem to like him that much.

They call him names
and make up jokes about his mum.

Everyone laughs . . . except Billy.
Everyone laughs . . . except Billy.

They all think it's OK
because it's only a laugh and a joke
and they don't really mean it anyway
but Billy doesn't know that.

Billy doesn't know that
and because of that
Billy doesn't like school really.

All I Want Is a Friend

All I want is a friend, the little girl said
A friend to sit with me in class
A friend to have dinner with
A friend to talk about last night's telly with

All I want is a friend, she said
As she sat down next to someone
Who didn't really like her

It Wasn't Me

It wasn't me, sir, honest, sir
It wasn't me, sir, it was him.
I wasn't with him, honest, sir
It was definitely him, sir
But I definitely wasn't with him, honest, sir.
Honest, sir, I'm telling the truth
It wasn't me, it was him, sir.
It can't have been me, sir
I wasn't with him.
Honest, sir.

I was quite near him though.

I Want to Be Bad

Darth Vader is my hero
I wish he was my dad
I just want to dress in black
I want to be bad! Ha-ha-ha-ha-haaa!

I pull the legs off spiders
And disembowel flies
I like to drop live earwigs
On my sleeping sister's eyes
I'm good at stretching slugs
I bite the shells off snails
Then put them on my sister's head
With all their sticky trails

Darth Vader is my hero
I wish he was my dad
I just want to dress in black
I want to be bad! Ha-ha-ha-ha-haaa!

I colour all her colouring books
With deepest darkest black
Wipe bogeys on the pages
Before I put them back
I twist the arms off baby dolls
And snap off teddy's head
Then cover it with ketchup
And leave it in her bed

Darth Vader is my hero
I wish he was my dad
I just want to dress in black
I want to be bad! Ha-ha-ha-ha-haaa!

I'm evil and I'm nasty
The best at being worst
If badness was a race
Then I would be the first
I fear nothing, no one
I'm master of my doom
But when my sister tells my mum . . .
I'm sent up to my room.

The Whoopee Cushion Waiting on the Teacher's Chair

All the class is silent – our eyes are fixed on where
The whoopee cushion's waiting on our teacher's chair

First she paces to the right, then paces to the left
Carries on the lesson while perching on her desk
Nobody is moving, everybody stares
At the whoopee cushion waiting on our teacher's chair

We're praying for that moment, when she will sit down
Thinking of the giggling when we hear that funny sound
SQUEAK! BLART! HONK! FLURP! PARP! BLURRR!
The whoopee cushion's waiting on our teacher's chair

What's that noise – bouncing down the corridor?
Mr Springer's coming and he's bouncing on the floor
We'd better all watch out, we'd better all beware
Cos the whoopee cushion's waiting on our teacher's chair

He's going to sit down on it! Oh no – disaster!
We're going to get in trouble now with our fat headmaster
It sounds like twenty tubas or a trumpet premiere
You should have seen him jump! Ten feet in the air!
A red-faced ranting raver – he began to swear
Sounds that shook the ground – vibrating everywhere
Sounds that bounced around – from behind his derrière
When the cushion was deflating on the teacher's chair

Everyone is frightened now, we're bound to get detention
But what happens next is beyond our comprehension
Mr Springer turns to Miss . . . and with an icy glare
He blames her for the whoopee cushion on the teacher's chair

Twice the embarrassment, twice the fun
Got two teachers for the price of one!
So much pleasure for us all to share . . .
Thanks to the whoopee cushion on the teacher's chair

Space Counting Rhyme

10 flying saucers, 10 flashing lights
9 glowing trails, 9 meteorites
8 silver spaceships trying to find
7 lost aliens left behind
6 burning comets blazing fire
5 red rockets blasting higher
4 satellites, 4 radar dishes
3 stars shooting means 3 wishes
2 bright lights – the moon and sun
1 little me to shine upon

Let No One Steal Your Dreams

Let no one steal your dreams
Let no one tear apart
The burning of ambition
That fires the drive inside your heart.

Let no one steal your dreams
Let no one tell you that you can't
Let no one hold you back
Let no one tell you that you won't.

Set your sights and keep them fixed
Set your sights on high
Let no one steal your dreams
Your only limit is the sky.

Let no one steal your dreams
Follow your heart
Follow your soul
For only when you follow them
Will you feel truly whole.

Set your sights and keep them fixed
Set your sights on high
Let no one steal your dreams
Your only limit is the sky.

Brace Yourself Tightly!

Mr Meacher – our head teacher
Very large and very round
Big red braces hold in place his
Baggy trousers, big and brown

All assembled, we all trembled
When his shouting turned to shaking
Frightened when his braces tightened
As his stomach started quaking

Most unsightly, stretching tightly
Until they could stretch no longer
What was next was unexpected
Shame his braces were not stronger

Buttons zinging, braces pinging
Everybody looked around
Bursting, popping, there's no stopping
Teacher's trousers falling down

Legs so wobbly, knees so knobbly
We could only sit and glance
At our head teacher Mr Meacher's
Pink and spotty underpants

Pink and spotty, pink and spotty
Very old and very grotty
Our head teacher Mr Meacher's
Pink and spotty underpants!

Mr Shadow's Shoes

Mr Shadow's shoes
Soft-soled shoes

Shush shush - left and right
Shush shush - out of sight

Mr Shadow's always there
No one knows exactly where
Soft-soled shoes
Silent on the stairs

Shush shush - left and right
Shush shush - out of sight

He's sneaking and he's creeping
He's spying and he's peeping
Soft-soled shoes
Are what he keeps his feet in

Shush shush - left and right
Shush shush - out of sight

Like a whisper near the door
Ghostly in the corridor
Soft-soled shoes
Slide across the floor

Shush shush - left and right
Shush shush - out of sight

Mr Shadow's shoes
Soft-soled shoes
Soft-soled silent shoes
Soft-soled slippy shoes
Soft-soled slidy shoes
Soft-soled shiny shoes
Mr Shadow's soft-soled slippy slidy shiny silent shoes

Shush shush – left and right
Shush shush – out of sight

He will always find you
Creeping up behind you
He will always find you
Look out . . . he's behind you

Shush shush – left and right
Shush shush – out of sight

Shush shush – left and right
Shush shush – out of sight

Shush shush – left and right
Shush shush – out of sight

Shush shush – left and right
Shush shush – out of sight

Shush shush – left and right
Shush shush – out of sight

When the Teacher Turns Their Back

Everyone's a maniac
When the teacher turns their back.

Books are toppled stack by stack
Worksheets scattered pack by pack
Lunches opened snack by snack
When the teacher turns their back.

Elastic bands go thwackety thwack
Pens and pencils clickety clack
Rulers twang and flickety flack
When the teacher turns their back.

Someone throws an anorak
Someone flies a plastic mac
Someone's chucking bric-a-brac
When the teacher turns their back.

Patak is whacking Mac and Jack
Matt is smacking Pat and Lak
Everyone's attacking Zack
When the teacher turns their back.

Rubbish scattered from the sack
Paint is splattered from the rack
Red and yellow, green and black
When the teacher turns their back.

Boys and girls have got the knack
A tug of war with stretched Blu-Tack
Six feet long and still no slack
When the teacher turns their back.

Victor thinks he's Vlad the Drac
Peter's riding piggyback
Nicola's a natterjack
When the teacher turns their back.

Karl's a kleptomaniac
Thinks it's clever to hijack
Kidnaps Katie's Caramac
When the teacher turns their back.

John looks like a frightened yak
Swinging from the curtain track
To and fro amidst the flak
When the teacher turns their back.

Yackety yackety yackety yak
Quackety quackety quackety quack
Everyone's a maniac
When the teacher – trusting creature –
When the teacher turns their back.

If All Else Fails – Buy the Teachers Chocolate

Always stand in silent line
Get your homework done on time
Never talk out of turn
Pretend that you just want to learn
Always do your writing neatly
Always concentrate completely
And if all else fails
buy the teachers . . . CHOCOLATE

Tidy up the playground toys
Never make a loud rude noise
Give out all the reading books
Compliment your teachers' looks
Tell your teachers they look nice
Even if you're telling lies
And if all else fails
buy the teachers . . . CHOCOLATE
lots and lots of CHOCOLATE

Or if it's Christmas or Easter time
Just buy them a great big bottle of . . .

It's Raining on the Trip

It's raining on the trip
Raining on the trip
Drip drip drip
Raining on the trip

It's never going to stop
Never going to stop
Drop drop drop
Never going to stop

I haven't got a coat
Haven't got a coat
Splish splash splosh
Going to get soaked

Under Ruth's waterproof
Under Pat's pakamac
Under Ella's umbrella
Under Mac's anorak
Things aren't getting much better
Things are getting much wetter

I think it's going to flood
Think it's going to flood
Thud thud thud
Think it's going to flood

The clouds are getting dark
Clouds are getting dark
If it rains much more
We're going to need an ark

It's raining on the trip
Raining on the trip
Drip drip drip
Raining on the trip

It's never going to stop
Never going to stop
Drop drop drop
Never going to stop

Miss King's Kong

It was our 'Bring your pet to school' day . . .

Warren's wolfhound was chasing Paula's poodle
Paula's poodle was chasing Colin's cat
Colin's cat was chasing Harriet's hamster
And Harriet's hamster was chasing Benny's beetle.

Suzie's snake was trying to swallow
Freddie's frog, Percy's parrot, Rebecca's rabbit,
Belinda's bat, Gordon's goat, Peter's pig
And part of Patricia's pony

When all of a sudden everything stopped.

Miss King had brought her pet to school as well.
Miss King's Kong stood there, roared and beat his chest.

Miss King smiled.
Miss King's Kong smiled too
As he swung from the light, eating bananas.

Everything was quiet
Until the headmaster came in with his pet . . .
Mr Lock's Ness was a real monster.

My Teacher's Great Big Tropical Fish Tank

My teacher's great big tropical fish tank is huge.
It fills up a whole wall in his classroom.

He changes the water regularly.
It's at exactly the right temperature.

There are pebbles, stones, deep-sea wrecks
and sunken treasure chests in the sand.

Plants waft gracefully in the gentle currents
and those little bubbles rise to the surface constantly.

Yes, my teacher's great big tropical fish tank is huge.
It covers up a whole wall in his classroom.

He hasn't got any tropical fish though . . .

Mind you, the guinea pigs seem quite happy.
They like the snorkels, masks and flippers.

Where Teachers Keep Their Pets

Mrs Cox has a fox
nesting in her curly locks.

Mr Spratt's tabby cat
sleeps beneath his bobble hat.

Mrs Cahoots has various newts
swimming in her zip-up boots.

Mr Spry has Fred his fly
eating food stains from his tie.

Mrs Groat shows off her stoat
round the collar of her coat.

Mr Spare's got grizzly bears
hiding in his spacious flares.

And . . .

Mrs Vickers has a stick insect called 'Stickers'
And she keeps it in her . . .

All Creatures Great and Small

All things bright and beautiful
All creatures great and small
All things live and wonderful
Our teacher hates them all

The spider in her teacup
The wasp inside her socks
The cockroach in the sandwich
The ants in her lunch box

The skunk stuck in the storeroom
The mouse inside her desk
The beetles in her trainers
And climbing up her dress

The caterpillars creeping
On to her new permed hair
The stick insects all sticking
In her underwear

The bumblebees that hide in
The pockets of her coat
The frogs inside her handbag
The lizard round her throat

All things bright and beautiful
All creatures great and small
We bring them and our teacher is
Frightened by them all

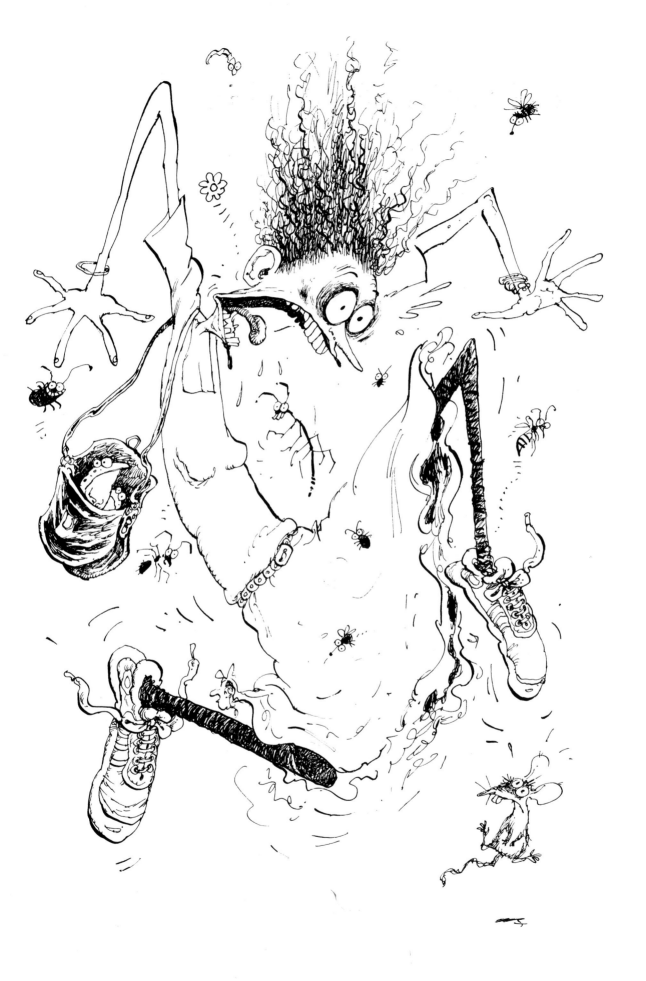

The noises that she screams out
The way she jumps up high
The way she runs round the room
The fear in her eyes

Like a cartoon human
She entertains the masses
She is wild and wonderful
Embarrassed in her classes

All things bright and beautiful
All creatures great and small
All things live and wonderful
Our teacher hates them all

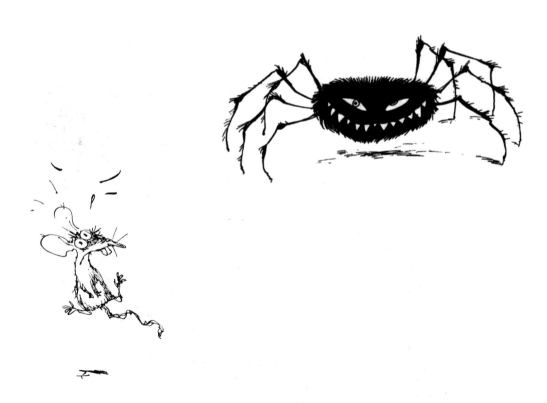

Short Visit, Long Stay

Our school trip was a special occasion
But we never reached our destination
Instead of the zoo
I was locked in the loo
Of an M62 service station.

Well-kept Secret

He lives inside my bedroom
My very special pet
I've had my skunk for five years now
And no one's noticed yet.

Bonkers for Conkers

I'm bonkers for conkers
I have a sixty-one-er
Billy's belter battered it
Now it is a goner.

My Uncle Percy Once Removed

My Uncle Percy once removed
his bobble hat, scarf, overcoat,
woolly jumper, string vest,
flared trousers and purple Y-fronts
and ran on to the pitch at Wembley
during a Cup Final
and was at once removed
by six stewards and nine officers of the law.
Once they'd caught him.

It's Not the Same Any More

It's not the same since Patch died,
Sticks are just sticks, never thrown, never fetched.
Tennis balls lie still and lifeless.
The urge to bounce them has gone.

It's not the same any more.
I can't bring myself to whistle – there's no reason to do so.
His collar hangs on the hook
And his name tag and lead are dusty.

His basket and bowl are in a plastic bag
Lying at an angle on the garage shelf.
My new slippers will never be chewed
And I've no excuse for my lack of homework any more.

I can now watch the football in peace, uninterrupted.
No frantic barking and leaping just when it gets to the goal.
I don't have to share my sweets and biscuits
And then wipe the dribbling drool off my trouser legs.

It's just not the same any more.
When Patch died, a small part of me died too.
All that's left is a mound of earth
And my handmade cross beneath the apple tree.

All that's left are memories. Thousands of them.
It's just not the same any more.

Richard

Richard was our friend.
For years.

You knew the best bands and newest records,
The goalscorers, grounds and team nicknames.
Always had some bit of useless but interesting information.
Always smiled that laid-back smile,
Always there with something good.
We laughed with you and joked with you.
We played football and guitar with you.
Until last year.

We cried when we heard.
Lots. And lots.
And lots. We still do.

So much of you to remember
So much life yet to live
So much we don't want to forget
So much more you had to give
So much we never said and did
So much of you lives on
So much of your light still shines
We can't believe you're gone

Richard was our friend.
One of the best.
Ever.

The Jumper Granny Knitted

The wool is rough and itchy
One sleeve is longer than the other
Teddies on the back
She thinks I am my little brother
It's shapeless and untrendy
Embarrassing, ill-fitted
I'm not going out like that . . .
In the jumper Granny knitted.

Thomas the Tank Engine on the front
Seventeen shades of green
She thinks that I'm still seven
When really I'm thirteen
Every Christmas, every birthday
She really is committed
I'm not going out like that . . .
In the jumper Granny knitted.

Don't worry, you'll grow into it!
It's the size of a family tent
And I was so much looking forward
To the present that she sent
Pretend that it's just perfect
And smile while teeth are gritted
I'm not going out like that . . .
In the jumper Granny knitted.

No way seen in public
For fear of ridicule
Too much humiliation
And never near my school
But whenever Granny comes to call
However wits are pitted
I'm not going out like that . . .
In the jumper Granny knitted.

I'm not going out like that
In the jumper Granny knitted.
I'd rather go in hiding
But that is not permitted
But you always have to wear it once
Or you may as well admit it . . .
That you hate and cannot stand
It makes you want to vomit and
You'd rather have one second-hand
Than . . . the jumper Granny knitted.
I'm not going out like that . . . in . . .
The jumper Granny knitted!

Mum for a Day

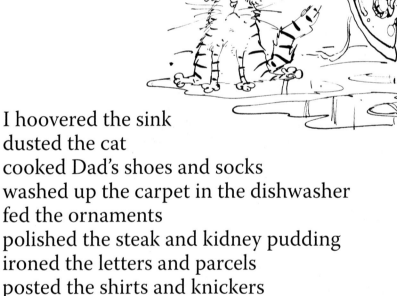

Mum's ill in bed today
so I said I'd do the housework
and look after things.
She told me it was really hard
but I said it would be dead easy
so . . .

I hoovered the sink
dusted the cat
cooked Dad's shoes and socks
washed up the carpet in the dishwasher
fed the ornaments
polished the steak and kidney pudding
ironed the letters and parcels
posted the shirts and knickers
and hung the budgie out to dry.

It took me all day but I got everything finished
and I was really tired
and I'm really glad Mum isn't ill every day.
So is the budgie.

Love Poem for ...

I just can't wait to be with you
Time flies by when you are there
You take me to another place
Just me and you and a comfy chair

You fill my head with images
And feelings I can't wait to share
You touch all my emotions
Just me and you and a comfy chair

Where you go I follow
You can take me anywhere
Horizons disappear with you . . .
A favourite book and a comfy chair.

Just Mum and Me

We didn't do anything special today,
just Mum and me.
Raining outside, nowhere to go,
just Mum and me.

So we baked and talked and talked and baked
and baked and talked,
just Mum and me.

She told me about when she was young
and how her mum baked exactly the same cakes
on rainy days and baked and talked to her.

She remembered her friends
and the games they used to play,
the trees they used to climb,
the fields they used to run around in
and how summers always seemed to be sunny.

And Mum smiled a smile I don't often see,
the years falling away from her face,
and just for a moment
I caught a glimpse of the girl she used to be.

We didn't do anything special today,
raining outside, nowhere to go,
so we baked and talked and talked and baked,
just Mum and me.

I ate and listened and listened and ate,
the hours racing by so quickly.

We didn't do anything special . . .
but it was special, really special.

Just Mum and me.

Father's Hands

Father's hands
large like frying pans
broad as shovel blades
strong as weathered spades.

Father's hands
finger ends ingrained with dirt
permanently stained from work
ignoring pain and scorning hurt.

I once saw him walk boldly up to a swan
that had landed in next door's drive and wouldn't move.
The police were there because swans are a protected species,
but didn't do anything, but my dad walked up to it,
picked it up and carried it away. No problem.
Those massive wings that can break a man's bones
were held tight, tight by my father's hands
and I was proud of him that day, really proud.

Father's hands
tough as leather on old boots
firmly grasping nettle shoots
pulling thistles by their roots.

Father's hands
gripping like an iron vice
never numb in snow and ice
nails and screws are pulled and prised.

He once found a kestrel with a broken wing
and kept it in our garage until it was better.
He'd feed it by hand with scraps of meat or dead mice
and you could see where its beak and talons
had taken bits of skin from his finger ends.
It never seemed to hurt him at all, he just smiled
as he let it claw and peck.

Father's hands
lifting bales of hay and straw
calloused, hardened, rough and raw
building, planting, painting . . . more.

Father's hands
hard when tanning my backside
all we needed they supplied
and still my hands will fit inside

Father's hands
large like frying pans
broad as shovel blades
strong as weathered spades.

And still my hands will fit inside
my father's hands.

Full of Surprises

This poem is full of surprises
Each line holds something new
This poem is full of surprises
Especially for you . . .

It's full of tigers roaring
It's full of loud guitars
It's full of comets soaring
It's full of shooting stars

It's full of pirates fighting
It's full of winning goals
It's full of alien sightings
It's full of rock and roll

It's full of rainbows beaming
It's full of eagles flying
It's full of dreamers dreaming
It's full of teardrops drying

It's full of magic spells
It's full of wizards' pointy hats
It's full of fairy elves
It's full of witches and black cats

It's full of dragons breathing fire
It's full of dinosaurs
It's full of mountains reaching higher
It's full of warm applause

It's full of everything you need
It's full of more besides
It's full of food, the world to feed
It's full of fairground rides

It's full of love and happiness
It's full of dreams come true
It's full of things that are the best
Especially for you

It's jammed and crammed and packed and stacked
With things both old and new
This poem is full of surprises
Especially for you.

Figuratively Speaking

If I speak in pictures
Then your ears must be my canvas
And my tongue a brush that paints the words
I want you to imagine.

Mum Used Pritt Stick

Mum used Pritt Stick
Instead of lipstick
Then went and kissed my dad.

Two days passed
Both stuck fast.
The longest snog they ever had.

First Kisses

First kisses are worrying.
What do you do?
Is there a right way of doing it?

Do you keep your lips dead tight
And rub them side by side?
Or do you leave them open
And let them go all squishy and wobbly?

Should you do sink-plunger impressions?
Is it safer to leave them open –
At least until you know
That you are not going to bang noses?

What happens if both your glasses steam up at the same time?
Or your braces get caught on theirs?

What about if you dribble?

Be careful if you sneeze . . .
You might blow their head off!
And what happens if you breathe in suddenly?

Whatever you do – and whoever you do it with,
Just remember this one important rule:
Make sure that the first person you ever ever kiss
Does not have a runny nose.

Trick or Treat

Trick or treat, trick or treat
Pumpkins light up every street
Trick or treat, trick or treat
Witches watch and gremlins greet
Trick or treat, trick or treat
Skeletons and vampires meet
Trick or treat or trick or treat

Halloween, Halloween
Ghosts and ghouls glowing green
Halloween, Halloween
Werewolves, hairy, scary, mean
Halloween, Halloween
Mummies lurch and monsters lean
Hallo Hallo Halloween.

The Day We Built the Snowman

Round and round the garden,
Rolling up the snow,
One step, two step,
Watch the snowman grow.

Round and round the garden,
Us and Dad and Mum,
Building up the snowman,
Having lots of fun.

Mum has got a carrot,
Dad has got a pipe,
Sister's got a scarf
To keep him warm at night.

Baseball cap and shades,
Trainers for his feet,
Our trendy friendly snowman,
The coolest in the street.

Round and round the garden
In the winter weather,
The day we built the snowman . . .
Having fun together.

Round and round the garden,
Rolling up the snow,
One step, two step,
Watch the snowman grow.

Round and round the garden,
Us and Dad and Mum,
Building up the snowman,
Having lots of fun.

The Last Day of Summer

Shadows lengthen one last time
Ice-cream vans hibernate
Shorts are banished to the bottom drawer
Cricket bats and tennis rackets revert to being pretend guitars.
Barbecues burn sausages no more
Shirtsleeves roll down, not up
And somewhere under the stairs
There is the rustling of warmer coats
As woollen gloves gently wake from slumber
Deep inside their padded-pocket nests.

The First Snow of Winter

Waking up to the scrunching carpet crunch,
the photographic negative,
the cotton-wool icing,
the transforming blanket
where even city centres could be Christmas cards
every child
delves in the understairs cupboard
for winter coats and wellies
wanting to be the first,
the very first, the very very first
to leave their mark, their print
and hear the sound of footprints in the snow.

I Wish I'd Been Present at Christmas Past

I wish I'd been a shepherd
and heard the angels sing.
I wish I'd been to Bethlehem
and seen the Infant King.

I wish I'd been a wise man
at the stable bare
following the star with
gold, frankincense and myrrh.

I wish I'd been an animal
who shared my manger hay
with that special newborn baby
on that first Christmas Day.

Stairway to the Clouds

I took a stairway to the clouds
And a camel to the moon
A trampoline to Timbuktu
And a rocket to my room

A skateboard to the Red Sea
A submarine to Mars
A freight train to Atlantis
I dived up to the stars

Parachuting on the ocean
I rode my bike down deep
I took a racing car to bed
And drove myself to sleep

I caught a bus that flew
To a bridge across the seas
And then in my canoe
I slalomed through the trees

I scootered on thin ice
Space-hoppered into space
With ice skates on the running track
I raced the human race

I bounced upon my pogo stick
All round the equator
I scaled the peak of Everest
Thanks to an elevator

I rope-swung in the city
Piggybacked through town
Rode horses down the rivers
Skied deep down underground

I swam across the deserts
And surfed on escalators
I roller-skated on glaciers
And leapfrogged high skyscrapers

I've travelled many places
In my different styles
Near and far and deep and wide
Millions of miles

But no matter how I wander
No matter where I roam
Of all these special journeys
The best one is . . . back home.

The Downhill Racers

Pushing pedals, setting paces
Wind-blown hair and smiling faces
Grinning, winning, speeding aces
We're the downhill racers

Great adventures, going places
Rocket ships to lunar bases
Motorcycle cops on chases
We're the downhill racers

Thrills and spills – faster, faster!
Gliding wheels sliding past you
Hear the squeals and shouts of laughter
We're the downhill racers

High-octane adrenalin pumping
Hammer pounding, heartbeat thumping
Wild excited jumping, bumping
We're the downhill racers

Wheels of fire – we're fanatics
On cloud nine – we're ecstatic
Mad for it – cyclopathic
We're the downhill racers

The urge to surge downhill's appealing
Nothing else can beat this feeling
Leading, speeding and freewheeling
We're the downhill

downhill

racers!

Just in Case

In assembly today we had a visit from the vicar.
I wasn't really listening,
I was thinking about that goal I scored last night
and then I thought about that girl from Class Six
   who's really nice
and how Muggo Mills is a bully and smells,
when I heard the vicar say
'. . . and God sees everything we do, boys and girls . . .'

I stopped thinking about goals and girls and grotbags.
Does that mean everything?
Does he see me pulling faces behind the teacher's back,
being cheeky to Mum,
blaming things on my little brother,
copying my homework off Jimbo,
giving the dog my teatime cabbage,
picking my nose and wiping it on the chair,
sitting on the loo . . . ?!?!

I hope he didn't see me laughing at that old lady
or the time I put the tortoise on roller skates.
Maybe he blinked when I put salt and pepper in boring
   Auntie Jean's tea.
Perhaps he wasn't looking when I called the new boy
   that horrible name . . .

Just in case he can see everything,
maybe I'll try a bit harder in the future.
Just for a bit anyway.
Just in case.

Footprints in the Sand

Footprints, footprints
Footprints in the sand
You and me, Lord, on the beach
Walking hand in hand
Side by side you walk with me
Through this barren land
Footprints, footprints
Footprints in the sand

I look and see the footprints
Footprints in the sand
Two souls entwined together
God's walk along with man
Then I glance and see a sight
I don't quite understand
Just one set of footprints
Footprints in the sand

You said that you would be with me
I followed your command
You left me all alone with pain
That I could not withstand
The time I needed you the most
My Lord, I must demand
Why just one set of footprints
Footprints in the sand?

The Lord looked down and smiled
With gentle reprimand
My son, this explanation
Everything is planned
I never left your side at all
And when you could not stand
That was when I carried you
Those footprints in the sand

Footprints, footprints
Footprints in the sand
You and me, Lord, on the beach
Walking hand in hand
Often you would carry me
Through this barren land
Footprints, footprints
Footprints in the sand

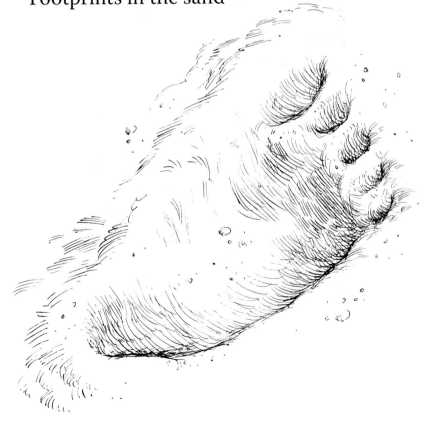

Wrigglebum John

Wrigglebum John
Wrigglebum John
He's got a chair that he won't sit on

Fidget left
Fidget right
Fidget through the day and night

Wrigglebum John
Wrigglebum John
He's got a chair that he won't sit on

Every day
Hour and minute
He's got a chair but he can't stay in it

On the tables watch him crawl
Climbing up and down the wall
Swinging on the lights and curtains
Of one thing you can be certain
Jumping running skipping hopping
You have not a chance of stopping

Wrigglebum John
Wrigglebum John
He's got a chair that he won't sit on

Now he's here
Now he's gone
Doesn't stay around for long

Where does he get his energy from?
Wrigglebum Wrigglebum Wrigglebum John
Wrigglebum Wrigglebum Wrigglebum John
Wrigglebum Wrigglebum Wrigglebum . . . JOHN!

A selected list of poetry titles available from Macmillan Children's Books

The prices shown below are correct at the time of going to press. However, Macmillan Publishers reserves the right to show new retail prices on covers, which may differ from those previously advertised.

The Works: Poems for the Literacy Hour
Chosen by Paul Cookson   978-0-330-48104-5   £6.99

The Works 3: A Poet a Week
Chosen by Paul Cookson   978-0-330-45181-9   £6.99

Give Us a Goal!
Football Poems by Paul Cookson   978-0-330-43654-0   £3.99

Pants on Fire
Poems by Paul Cookson   978-0-330-41798-3   £3.99

All Pan Macmillan titles can be ordered from our website, www.panmacmillan.com, or from your local bookshop and are also available by post from:

Bookpost, PO Box 29, Douglas, Isle of Man IM99 1BQ
Credit cards accepted. For details:
Telephone: 01624 677237
Fax: 01624 670923
Email: bookshop@enterprise.net
www.bookpost.co.uk

Free postage and packing in the United Kingdom